MCR

AUG 0 3 2004

EVANSTON P   P9-CBS-300

3 1192 01253 8668

JPicture Stadl.A

Stadler, Alexander.

Lila Bloom /

c2004.

For Darrin Britting and Jamie Bishton

PRONUNCIATION GUIDE

plié, pliés: plee-ay

grand jeté: grahn zheh-tay

barre: bar

ronds de jambe: ron deh zhahmb

développés: day-vell-oh-pay

pirouette: pee-roo-wett

tour jeté: toor zhe-tay

piqué: pee-kay

pas de chat: pah de shah

La classe est finie: la clahss ay fee-nee

révérence: reh-vuh-ronse

fantastique: fahn-tas-teek

Copyright © 2003 by Alexander Stadler
All rights reserved
Distributed in Canada by Douglas & McIntyre Ltd.
Color separations by Chroma Graphics PTE Ltd.
Printed and bound in the United States of America by Berryville Graphics
Designed by Nancy Goldenberg
First edition, 2004
10 9 8 7 6 5 4 3 2 1

Library of Congress Cataloging-in-Publication Data
Stadler, Alexander.
    Lila Bloom / Alexander Stadler.— 1st ed.
        p.   cm.
    Summary: Angry after a difficult day, Lila decides to quit ballet class but reconsiders after she realizes that dancing makes her feel much better.
    ISBN 0-374-34474-4
    [1. Anger—Fiction.   2. Ballet dancing—Fiction.]   I. Title.

PZ7.S7754 Li 2004
[E]—dc21
                                                        2002035312

Lila Bloom

ALEXANDER STADLER

EVANSTON PUBLIC LIBRARY
CHILDREN'S DEPARTMENT
1703 ORRINGTON AVENUE
EVANSTON, ILLINOIS 60201

Frances Foster Books

Farrar, Straus and Giroux / New York

$\mathcal{L}$ila Bloom was having a miserable day.

At breakfast, everyone else's waffle had at least ten strawberries.
Lila's waffle had only one.

Her little sister smeared maple syrup all over her favorite sweatshirt.
Lila had to wear a party dress to school.

In school, the girl sitting next to her got a gold star on her book report. Lila's paper said "Try Harder."

By the time the bell rang at the end of the day, Lila was really grumpy. She was in such a bad mood that she wasn't even looking forward to her ballet class. As she climbed into her Aunt Celeste's shiny little sports car, she scowled.

"I despise ballet," she muttered as she punched in her seat belt. "It's ridiculous. Up down. Up down. Plié this. Grand jeté that. Jump here. Leap there. The shoes, the stupid tutus—the whole thing makes me sick. How I wish I could quit!"

Aunt Celeste, hiding a small smile, kept her eyes on the road.

"In fact, nothing would make me happier than never having to see that stinky old rehearsal hall again."

"If that's really how you feel," said Aunt Celeste, still keeping a close watch on the traffic, "why don't you just finish today's class, and then you'll never have to go again."

In the dressing room, Lila made her announcement.
"I am quitting," she said in a loud voice. "This will be my last class."

"Are you really quitting?" asked one of the other girls.

"Sure am," said Lila.

There was a flurry of excitement and chatter, but it all came to an end when they heard Madame Vera banging her stick and calling them to the floor.

They quickly assembled at the barre. Only Lila walked a little slower than the rest.

Madame Vera had been a prima ballerina with the Hungarian Classical Ballet. "Let us begin," she said.

Lila was noticeably distracted. Her pliés were shallow.

Her ronds de jambe lacked finesse.

Her développés were underdeveloped.

Lila could feel Madame Vera watching her. But instead of returning her teacher's gaze, she pretended to focus on something out the window and far away.

The class moved to the center of the floor. Lila was in the middle of a lazy pirouette when Madame Vera took her by the shoulders and looked her straight in the eyes.

"Is Mademoiselle not feeling well today?" she asked.

"No, I'm fine," answered Lila. "It's just that today is my last day. I'm quitting ballet."

"Perhaps that is why Mademoiselle Bloom has been dancing like an old noodle?"

Lila didn't know what to say.

"Maybe it is for the best, then," said Madame, lifting Lila's chin so she could speak right to her face. "Mademoiselle Bloom has not been dancing that well, anyway."

The other pupils began to whisper. With a bang of her stick, a little louder than usual, Madame called out, "Let us continue!"

The class began to move across the floor. Lila stood at the back of the line. Her face was beet red and her thoughts were going a mile a minute.

"That old goose!" she thought to herself. "She knows I'm the second-best dancer in the class. I'll show her. I'll be ten times as good today, and then she'll really miss me when I'm gone."

Lila looked up. She had reached the head of the line. She leaped. Anger made her grand jeté even grander than usual. She made sure to land without a sound. Madame Vera did not even look at her.

"That blind bat!" thought Lila. "This will get her attention!"

She executed a perfect tour jeté. When she landed, Madame was paying attention to someone else.

Lila spun through her piqué turns with strength and delicacy. She made her pas de chat with the utmost grace. Madame didn't even seem to notice.

And then something interesting happened . . .

As Lila concentrated on her dancing, it became harder to stay angry. It stopped mattering to her whether Madame was looking or was not.

The more she danced,
the happier she became.
By the end of class, all
she could think of was
the music from the piano
and how it seemed to be
moving her across the floor.

It was almost like waking up from a dream when she heard the banging of the stick and Madame's voice saying solemnly, *"La classe est finie."*

After the class made their révérence, bowing to their teacher and shaking her hand, Lila gathered up her things in a daze.

As she walked toward the lockers, Madame Vera touched her shoulders and said, "It is a shame that Mademoiselle is leaving us, as her work today was really quite good."

"Oh no, madame! I've changed my mind. In fact, would it be possible for me to join the Saturday class as well?"

"Hmmm," said Madame Vera. "Let me see about making a place for you."
Lila grabbed her things and went out to the curb. Aunt Celeste was
waiting for her.

"How was class?" she asked as Lila climbed into the car.

"Excellent!" said Lila. *"Fantastique!* I even spoke to Madame Vera about taking two classes a week instead of one. Do you think that would be all right?"

"I think it's a great idea—and about time," answered Aunt Celeste. "In fact, I think we should go to Luigi's Luncheonette and celebrate. I'm in the mood for a chocolate malted. What are you going to have?"

"I'm going to have a strawberry banana parfait," said Lila, "with extra everything." And then she sat back in her seat and she smiled.